OFF THE RAILS

D1437502

The train juddered and pulled itself back into action. Karl watched the car, the only patch of colour, as it shrank to a dot. As the train started to rumble along the track, he glanced back at the dyke. The carpet was loosely rolled, as though bundled around something. It had come partly undone as it fell down the slope of the dyke. And there, sticking out of the end, was a leg, ending in a scruffy trainer.

OFF THE RAILS

Anne Rooney

Published by Evans Brothers Limited
2A Portman Mansions
Chiltern St
London W1U 6NR

First published in 2010.

British Library Cataloguing in Publication Data
Rooney, Anne.
  Off the rails. -- (Shades)
  1. Suspense fiction. 2. Young adult fiction.
  I. Title II. Series
  823.9'2-dc22

  ISBN-13: 9780237541347

Editor: Julia Moffatt
Designer: Rob Walster

Chapter One

Karl stared out at the flat, black landscape of the Fens as the train clattered and lurched along. Rain streaked the windows, so that fat drops slanted across his field of vision, blurring the dull view. Nearly home. His iPod was out of battery and he'd eaten the crisps he'd bought on the way from school to the station. Daniel, sitting next to him, was silent and messing with his phone, texting some girl he'd met at half term. The fat woman opposite huffed and puffed and shifted in her seat – in both the seats she filled. And Karl stared out of the window.

The wide ditches ran like deep cuts through the fields here. Green banks on either side, the lips of these great wounds, rose up to the edge and then the ditch – dykes they were called, weren't they? – the dyke severed one field from the next. In the nearest field, a band of bedraggled and drenched migrant workers stooped over, picking onions. Karl couldn't see their gang-master.

Daniel looked up from texting the girl he was after.

'Losers,' he said. 'Look at them. They live in caravans and spend their days scouring the mud for shitty onions. Why don't they stay at home? At least it might be sunny at home.'

Karl stared at the line of workers. Perhaps they were losers. But his life didn't seem much more exciting than theirs just now. A long round of GCSE coursework and arguments with his parents and the endless train journeys to and from school. He couldn't wait to leave in the summer – four months to go. He was practically counting the days. Then he saw her. She raised her head, glanced unseeing towards the train, pushed her long, black hair back over her shoulders and put a hand to the small of her back.

'Look!' Karl poked Daniel, who had turned back to his phone. 'Isn't that the girl we met on Saturday? At the market? Eleni?'

Daniel lifted his head again, but they were too far past to be sure.

'Nah, can't be.'

'It could be. Her friend, she didn't speak much English. Remember? They spoke together in Serbian or something. If they're migrants camping on the farm that would be why they wouldn't say where they live.'

Daniel ignored him, pressing the buttons on his phone in quick succession.

The train was slowing, stopping. Karl kept his face close to the window. A dyke just a few metres away was clogged with rubbish: an old fridge-freezer, a broken supermarket trolley, a pet basket. There was a battered, red estate car drawn up close to it and a swarthy man opening the hatch. More rubbish, no doubt. Another man, wiry and blond, got out of the passenger side and between them they

hauled something long and heavy out of
the boot. Now the train was still, the rain
pounded on the window and ran straight
down. It turned the scene outside into a
rippling blur as though someone had
poured acid over it and fuzzied the edges.
The thing was a rolled-up carpet. The
men dumped it at the top of the dyke,
and it rolled and slithered down the slope.
Without looking back, the men jumped
back in the car, then sped off, the tyres
slipping once on the muddy road.

The train juddered and pulled itself back
into action. Karl watched the car, the only
patch of colour, as it shrank to a dot. As
the train started to rumble along the track,
he glanced back at the dyke. The carpet
was loosely rolled, as though bundled
around something. It had come partly
undone as it fell down the slope of the

dyke. And there, sticking out of the end, was a leg, ending in a scruffy trainer.

Karl's skin prickled and his hands sweated.

'Daniel! Look!' He grabbed his friend's arm, but Daniel shook him off.

'I'm busy,' he grumbled.

'But look! It's important!'

Daniel sighed and leaned over Karl to look out of the window. Karl felt him tense as he saw the foot.

'Shit,' said Daniel.

The fat woman shuffled her bulk and tutted under her breath. Karl looked over at her.

'Did you see that? In the dyke?'

It took her a moment to realise he was talking to her, then she glanced out of the window, but the dyke was disappearing from view.

'People's always dumping rubbish in the

dykes. It's a scandal.'

'But the carpet—' he began.

'Did you see the carpet?' Daniel added. 'And the leg? Did you see a leg?' He was on the edge of his seat now, his phone forgotten in his hand.

'All kinds. They dumps all kinds. It's a scandal,' she repeated. She wasn't really listening, or she hadn't really looked. Daniel opened his mouth to try again, but Karl shook his head. There was nothing to see now.

Karl turned back to the rainy window while she jabbered on. He carried on staring even when the dyke and its bundle lay far behind them. Every now and then, Daniel caught his eye in their reflections in the window.

Chapter Two

At last the train pulled into the station. Karl and Daniel hurried through the ticket barrier.

'Do you think we should go to the police?' Karl asked.

'Yes. But you go,' said Daniel. 'They won't believe you if I go – I was threatened with an ASBO for making those hoax calls with Barnie – remember? '

'But—' Karl began.

'No, really, I'd better not. Let me know, right? Seeya.'

Karl unlocked his bike and cycled to the police station as fast as the weather allowed, his tyres spraying water on angry pedestrians. Once there, he stood outside in the rain for a moment. Was he really going to report a murder? How did this work? Would it be like it is on TV? It was exciting. He felt his heart beating hard in his chest as he pushed open the glass door.

He told the officer at the desk what he'd seen. The man looked bored.

'So it's a carpet in a dyke, you say?'

'It's got a body in it. There's a leg sticking out.'

'You're sure about that, are you? You're not messing about?'

'No. I really saw it. Honestly, I did.'

'OK. We'll get a car down there to take a look.' The man sighed, and took Karl's details. 'We'll call you if we need anything.'

Was that it? How disappointing. Karl cycled home, replaying in his head what he'd seen through the window, reconstructing the men, the car, the carpet – looking for anything he'd missed.

There was nothing on the news about a missing person or the police finding a body. It was nine thirty before his phone rang.

'Is that Karl Fitzsimons? Just following up your crime report. There's no body at the site, just a discarded carpet…'

But the leg, Karl thought. What about the leg?

Chapter Three

'What's your name, girl?'

'Eleni.'

'I don't like your sort. I don't want your sort here. I told your father and his friends not to come. I came to this country for a new start, without your murdering troop, and if you put one foot out of line, you'll pay the price. You can disappear, just like people disappeared from the villages back home.' He grabbed her arm, easily circling it.

'I was just a child. I don't know anything about it,' she said, twisting away.

He tightened his grip.

'Watch your step, or you'll be next.'

'I've done nothing—'

'Shut it.'

The man's thin fingers dug into the flesh of her arm, making her wince. He pushed her, hard, so that she stumbled over the rutted mud of the field. She spat at him – it was a mistake. He lunged at her, and she took a step backwards.

'Get back to work and keep your trap shut,' he hissed at her. He pushed lank, blond hair back from his face.

'I'll be back for you later,' he added, and the edge of his mouth curled up in an ugly half-smile.

Eleni rubbed at her bare arm and stooped to pick onions out of the ground. She shivered. Her thin vest top was no protection against the bitter East Anglian wind of early morning. She knew he meant what he said. Her friend Catarina had vanished, gone without a word. At home, no one was safe. People from both sides disappeared. Sometimes they were found dead in the forests; often they just went away for ever. Last year, after the winter thaw, they found thirty bodies in a shallow pit a few miles from her village. That was when her father had urged her to leave. She and Catarina, smuggled out, suffocating in the back of a lorry, off to start a new life. And what a life it had turned out to be. They were no safer here, after all. What could she do? There was nowhere to run. She'd just have to keep her head down and hope he forgot about her.

Much later, as she worked at the end of the line of onion-pickers, the blond man stepped out in front of her.

'You know what this is?'

He held out a keyring, with a heart dangling from it. The heart was made of a jelly-like plastic substance, it was see-through, with a sickly pink tint, and had a tiny white plastic dog in the middle.

'It's Catarina's,' she said. Catarina had bought it on Saturday at the market. They'd had a good time, met a couple of boys, had a few drinks – it seemed years ago.

'*Was* Catarina's,' he corrected her. He threw it on to the mud. As she stooped to pick it up a hand clamped over her mouth. Eleni struggled, but another muscular hand held her tight.

'Right,' said a voice, low and harsh in her ear. 'Enough. You can go too. We'll get a good price for you two.' She stared wide-eyed at the backs of the other workers retreating across the fields. No one turned round.

Chapter Four

When the train passed the same spot in the morning, it was going faster. Karl pressed his forehead to the window, determined not to miss it. There was the dyke: no carpet. The police must have moved it. All day at school he tried to forget about it, but on the train home he found himself in the same seat again, waiting. Usually he and Daniel would talk, or fight, or start their homework, or play on their phones, but today Karl couldn't settle to anything. He just looked out of the window.

He saw a red car speeding across the fens away from the railway line. And then the train flashed by the dyke, and there was the carpet.

'Look!' he shouted. 'It's there!'

Daniel leaned forward and peered out of the window. He barely caught sight of it before they were past it.

'Still there, then,' he said.

'But it wasn't there this morning,' said Karl. 'Why would it come and go? Who would dump a carpet twice in the same place? We could go and check it out – we don't have anything else to do.'

'OK. Guess so. Maybe there's something

exciting wrapped in it. Money or stolen stuff. Maybe it's drugs,' said Daniel. 'Better be careful not to get our prints on it.'

It took a good fifteen minutes to cycle from the station to the dyke. The carpet was still there, lying in the mud, its ugly blue and green pattern smeared and smirched. Karl threw his bike down by a low wall and scrambled to the top of the dyke. Daniel arrived at his side a few moments later.

Karl missed his footing and slipped in the mud, landing on the rolled carpet. There were two noises. One was the soft thud of a fully grown boy stumbling on to a carpet. The other was a muffled moan. Karl froze.

'Idiot,' said Daniel, coming more carefully down the side of the dyke.

'Shhh!' hissed Karl. 'There's someone in there.'

'Dead people don't care if you make a

noise,' said Daniel. 'Look. *Whhoooo hooo* – dead person! Come and get me!'

'Shut up. They're not dead. Didn't you hear? When I landed on the carpet, it moaned.'

They both stood silently for a moment. Nothing.

'Is there anyone there?' Karl asked at last. They strained their ears. There *was* a moan.

'Let's get them out!' said Karl.

'Wait.' Daniel grabbed Karl's arm. 'We might need evidence. I'll get my phone and we'll take a picture first.'

'Hurry!'

Chapter Five

The carpet was bound in two places with duct tape. Karl felt in his pocket for his penknife, but of course he didn't have it – not allowed at school. He looked around for something sharp. There were some bits of broken plate in the dyke. He stooped over to pick one up and felt the rough edge with his finger. It would do.

'We'll get you out of there. Don't worry,' he said to the carpet. He knew you should talk to accident victims to keep them calm. Perhaps it was the same for people rolled up in a carpet. 'It won't be long. You'll be out soon.'

Daniel had clambered out of the dyke and hurried back to his bike. He fished around in his bike bag for his phone, feeling for it with his fingers amongst his books and PE kit, and he was bending over when he heard the voices. He ducked down, out of view. But it was too late for Karl.

'What are you doing here?'

Karl spun round. There was a stocky man with cropped, bristly, dark hair. He had a tattoo on one arm and held a car jack in his hand. Just behind him was another man, who somehow looked foreign. He was thin and blond, with a pinched face and scaly, flaking skin. Eczema, Karl thought.

'I was just – I don't know. Nothing. I was cycling home. That's all.'

'Always talk to carpets, do you?' The man tossed the car jack from one hand to the other. 'Well?'

'There was – there was a noise. I was just wondering—' Karl's mouth was dry. The man tossed the car jack between his hands again. The blond man said something that Karl couldn't understand and the stocky man looked at his watch. Then he made a dive for Karl and caught him by the arm. As Karl struggled, the man raised the car jack above his head. He started to bring his arm down, fast.

'OK, OK. Don't hurt me. What do you want?'

The blow glanced off Karl's shoulder, sending a searing pain through his arm and chest. The man raised the jack again and held it poised for a moment.

'Stop, please!'

'You should mind your own business,' the man said. But he didn't hit him again. 'We don't like people snooping around. Know what happens to kids that snoop around? Vladan, keep him quiet.'

The blond man, Vladan, took a roll of duct tape from his pocket. He taped up Karl's mouth and pulled his arms behind his back. Karl cried out in pain, but it sounded like a muffled moan. The muffled moan he had heard from inside the carpet. He felt sick as he realised what that meant. And then he thought: Where's Daniel?

Chapter Six

The dark man pushed him over on the
mud. Karl couldn't put his arms out to save
himself and he landed with a hard thud,
jarring his hip. The blond man taped his
ankles together. Karl started to kick out,
but saw the car jack raised again and lay
still. He couldn't breathe. He sucked air in

through his nostrils, making a snuffling sound. What if he suffocated? He looked around wildly, but the men were behind him now and he couldn't see them.

'I cut?' Vladan said.

Karl felt sick. What would they do to him? As soon as he felt sick, he felt even more scared. What if he were sick with his mouth taped closed? He'd heard of people who choked to death on their own vomit. He began to struggle, squirming on the ground. The dark man turned and kicked him in the back, making Karl suck in a huge gasp of air through his nostrils.

'Yes,' said the man. 'Cut. Now.'

Vladan walked back into Karl's field of view, holding a long knife. Karl's insides turned to liquid. What if they cut him and he couldn't scream? Daniel wouldn't know they were hurting him. But the man walked

past him and bent over the carpet. He slit
the duct tape and pulled the carpet away.
Karl saw long dark hair spilling like oil into
the mud, and then a scared face, the mouth
sealed with duct tape as he knew it would
be, and the cheeks smeared with make-up
that had run, and tears. The girl whimpered.
She looked familiar, but Karl couldn't see
her clearly. Vladan slapped her face and
held the knife to her throat.

'You shut it, yes?'

She nodded, fixing her eyes on him.
Vladan nodded too, and gave a nasty
sneer.

'See? You shouldn't have come here. I
told you. Gypsy scum. You should have
stayed in the forests eating squirrels.'

The girl looked over at Karl now, and
her eyes registered recognition at the same
time as he saw her properly. *Eleni.* Karl's

stomach turned a somersault. Vladan caught her looking at him and grabbed her face, turning it back towards himself.

'You like boys? We'll find boys for you. You'll get plenty boys where you're going. The more the merrier.' He made a rude gesture with his fingers.

'Get her in the car,' the dark man said. 'You picked a good one there – she'll be pretty when we clean her up. We'll get good money for her.'

Vladan stuck his hands under the girl's arms and hauled her out of the carpet and up the bank, her taped legs trailing in the mud. Karl couldn't see what was happening once she was out of the dyke, but he could hear them drag her and soon he heard a car door slam. What now? Would they drive away?

In seconds, they were back.

'Kill him?' said Vladan, waving his knife.

'No, you psycho,' said the dark man, but he laughed. 'We might get a decent price for him – there are people that like boys, nice muscly, blond boys like him. I know someone who'll take him. Stick him in the carpet. There'll be a train along in four minutes. We've got to get out of here.'

Rough hands pushed Karl on to the carpet and rolled it around him. He heard the tearing of the duct tape.

'Put in car?' It was Vladan.

'Not now; there's no room. We'll come back for him.'

Karl felt himself roll over and over as Vladan pushed the carpet into the dyke with his foot. Then he heard the men hurry away, car doors slam, an engine rev and roar and then slowly die away until he heard nothing.

A minute passed. Where the hell was Daniel? Karl realised he wouldn't know how long he was in there, and started to count in his head, slowly. He got to 135 when the roar of a train overhead startled him. And it was that which broke his spirit. Even if anyone on the train saw the carpet and reported it, the police wouldn't come now because they came yesterday. He squeezed his eyes closed, but tears still leaked out. Sixteen years old and crying like a baby, he thought.

A few seconds passed, then he heard footsteps. He held his breath.

'Karl?' It was Daniel. Karl struggled to move, to speak. He made a muffled grunt, but he knew it wasn't loud enough.

'Shit. You've gone. OK. Whoever you are in the carpet – I'll get you out.'

He scrambled down the bank and tried

to pull at the duct tape circling the carpet. It was impossible to break the tough plastic. The ends were invisible, somewhere underneath the roll. He shoved against the bulk of it but couldn't move it up the bank. Inside the carpet, Karl struggled to make Daniel hear him, but it was no use.

'I can't do it. I'm going to get the police. Those bastards have taken my mate. I won't forget you're here,' Daniel said. Karl heard Daniel's footsteps, and then nothing.

Chapter Seven

It was hard to breathe inside the carpet.
The dust made Karl want to cough, and
that made him feel he was suffocating
again. And it was hot. His throat was
parched. He felt panic rising like bile into
his mouth, and squirmed uselessly. If he
opened his eyes, they filled with dust and

he could see nothing anyway. His arms ached, and his bruised shoulder was throbbing. He'd stopped counting. His mind filled with thoughts of what might happen next. Then he heard the splashing of wheels through muddy puddles. They were back.

Karl felt himself hauled up. Someone had his head and someone had his feet, but his middle sagged down in the carpet. He was going head first, upwards, then along. He started counting again, counting the paces his captors took once they were on level ground. They dropped him, pushed him, rolled him. And then he was still. This time he was somewhere flat, but curled round a bit. There was a thud – must be a car door shutting – and then an engine starting up and they were off, slowly at first but soon speeding along, straight as an arrow over the fen roads. He started counting again. It distracted him from the panic, and if he could count the seconds between turns it might help to work out later where he had been taken. If he ever got out. If there was ever anyone to tell. He began to feel sick again. No. No. He had to be calm. Count. Just count.

He clenched his fists. *Ouch.* There was a sharp pain in his hand. Why? Of course! He was still holding the shard of plate – he'd forgotten all about it. He no longer felt it until he'd tightened his fingers around it, when it must have cut him. Karl wriggled his hand until he managed to get the shard between thumb and finger. He moved it along so that he held an edge. Carefully, slowly, he shifted it so that the part that had cut him was against the duct tape. He could barely move it, there was no way of sawing though the tape. He felt despair welling up again. No. Keep calm.

Which way up was he? He couldn't tell. There was a trick explorers used if they were caught in an avalanche, he'd read about it. Pee and see which way it runs through the snow. He wasn't about to pee himself – though now he thought about it, he did need to pee. He rolled his tongue around to gather some spit, but it was difficult as his mouth was so dry. He tried to dribble his meagre collection from the front of his mouth, but the tape was too tight. He remembered he'd cried. That would do. He opened his eyes and forced himself to keep them open until the dust and the dry air made them water. Tears trickled down each side of his head towards his ears. So he was face up – good. With huge effort, he stabbed the shard of plate down into the carpet, then moved his bound hands above it and pressed down. Nothing happened. He couldn't move his hands far enough to get any real pressure. Suddenly, the car bumped furiously and Karl heard Vladan swear as he struggled to keep it straight. The level crossing – fine at low speeds, but murder if you were strapped up in the boot of a car going way too fast. The last bump shook Karl hard – hard enough for him to feel a sharp pain as the fragment of plate cut through the tape and stabbed into his wrist. Yes!

He pulled his arms apart, wincing as the tape ripped the hairs from his wrists. With effort, he shuffled his arms round to his sides. His shoulders ached – he hadn't noticed how much they hurt until he could move again. The piece of plate dug sharply into his back, and Karl moved a hand round to pull it out of the carpet. By wriggling his arm he managed to reach up to his face to peel the tape from his mouth. The first thing he tasted was carpet dust, and the second was the salty blood on his fingers.

He didn't have time to congratulate himself. The car braked suddenly, and made a sharp left turn, throwing Karl first forward and then to one side. A minute later, it screeched to a halt and the doors slammed one after another as the men got out. Karl sealed the tape over his mouth again and, with difficulty, pushed his arms back behind him. He didn't want them to know he'd cut himself free if they took a look. There was nothing he could do about the blood.

'Quick, stick it down there with the girls!' It was the dark man's voice.

Again he was hauled out, and this time the carpet dropped from a height on to a hard floor. Karl cried out, but the noise was muffled by the tape and the carpet. No one took any notice. There was another noise, low and faint but rhythmic, getting louder – helicopter blades. Karl felt sick again. If they took him in a helicopter, there'd be no chance of tracking his route – they could take him anywhere.

'We go?' It was Vladan.

'Wait – torch the place! They'll search the building rather than chase us. Go!'

The man had to shout loudly to make his voice heard over the thundering of the chopper.

A few seconds later, a car engine roared – a different engine, Karl thought – and he heard a screech of tyres and a vehicle driving off.

Karl moved his hands back round to his sides and forced his way up to the top of the carpet roll, his head finally pushing out of the end. He looked around. Two girls huddled in a corner together; one was Eleni. They whimpered behind the duct tape over their mouths, their eyes wide with fear. Neither looked at him. He turned his head to look where they were looking. Flames lapped lazily over a pile of old newspapers and blankets.

Chapter Eight

The noise of the chopper was deafening now, making it hard for Karl to think. At least they weren't taking him in it. Perhaps it had come to pick up the men. The flames were still idling over the rubbish. They were far enough away for now. He pulled himself further out of the carpet. It was hard, with his legs still bound together and he got stuck. But half his body was out now. With the broken plate, he sliced through the tape round the carpet and wriggled, trying to roll it over. It didn't work. It was getting uncomfortably hot, even though the flames were not near him. Smoke stung his eyes and nose and made him cough. The girls' whimpering grew louder and they wriggled and struggled. They were closer to the fire than he was.

'It's OK,' he yelled to them, 'I'll get you out.'

But his voice was swallowed by the thundering noise of the helicopter. Eleni mumbled through the tape but he couldn't understand what she said.

At last Karl managed to haul himself out of the carpet and cut his legs free. He gave the carpet a heavy kick with his foot, so that it unrolled over the floor. He hoped it would cover the fire and put it out, but it stopped short, most of it still rolled. Sparks flew into the air and started to settle elsewhere on the ground, setting wisps of dry straw alight.

Karl ran to the girls and cut through the tape holding their arms and legs. He hauled Eleni to her feet, pointed at the door and pushed. She hesitated, staring at the flames starting to trickle across the opening.

Suddenly, the noise got much louder as the chopper banked and turned, sweeping low over the building, then started to lift and move away. But just as the noise started to drop again, the gust from the banking helicopter hit the barn, blowing the doors wide open. The blast took the flames and threw them around the building.

They leapt in all directions, ten times the size they were just seconds before.

'Get out!' Karl yelled at Eleni as he pulled the other girl to her feet. Neither moved. Then Eleni took a step backwards towards the wall, away from the fire, but also away from the door. The heat was searing Karl's face and hands now. They had only seconds, barely that long, to get out. And yet the girls wouldn't move.

'Go!' he screamed. 'Go now or we'll all die!' His throat was raw and burning. He'd used the last of his breath shouting at them. Karl started to choke, the smoke filling his mouth, his nose, his throat and his lungs. If they didn't move, he'd have to leave them. Everything seemed to slow down. Karl saw specks of red whirling in the smoke. He saw how his fingers dug into Eleni's arm making a white mark, but how the skin was reddening around them from the heat. He noticed the noise of the chopper fading, and the crackling of the fire growing louder. He thought he could pick out a different noise, rising and falling. Yes – the wailing of a siren. Hope flooded back and with a superhuman effort, he grabbed an arm in each hand and dragged the two girls towards the opening, though it was filled with flames. Then they finally started to move, forcing action from legs stiffened by hours lying bound up, and tearing the tape from their mouths.

He dragged and pulled at the girls as they stumbled. Flames licked around Eleni's jeans and she began to scream. Still he pulled her on, hauling her into and through the wall of flame and, at last, out on to the mud. He pushed Eleni over.

'Run!' he screamed between coughs at

the other girl, but she froze, staring at him and Eleni. Karl scooped a handful of mud and slapped it on Eleni's burning jeans. At least they were wet and weren't burning quickly. The flames were gone instantly. But the heat from the barn just behind was burning Karl's back. They were all gasping for breath, choking still on the smoke, but Karl knew they still had to move.

'We've got to get away,' he tried to say, but a coughing fit robbed him of the words. He grabbed Eleni's arm again and hauled her to her feet, and the three of them stumbled a few paces before falling on to cold, wet mud. The blaring of the sirens filled his ears and his mind, and smoke filled his lungs. Karl closed his eyes and let the blackness take over.

Chapter Nine

'OK, now mate, OK.' Karl opened his eyes. A policeman was cradling his head. Only seconds had passed. He sat up, and the policeman put a restraining hand on his shoulder. Karl took huge gulps of damp, cool air and started choking again.

'We'll get you some oxygen soon, mate.'

Karl waved a hand as though he could brush the words aside. He looked over towards the girls, who still stumbled over the rutted mud of the ground, coughing and crying. They clung together and spoke quickly in a language Karl didn't understand but had heard before. Another police officer was talking into his radio and looking towards the barn. The corner was now a column of flame, and smoke billowed in a giant mushroom cloud.

A second police car screeched to a halt beside the first. Daniel climbed out of the back and ran towards them. His instinct was to hug Karl – he was so pleased to see him alive. Instead, he clapped him on the shoulder. Karl flinched – the blow from the car jack had left a heavy bruise.

'Well done! What happened?' Daniel demanded.

'We'll need statements from you both,'
interrupted the driver from the second
police car. 'But first I want you all to move
well away from this building. If there's a
fuel store in there it could go up like a
bomb. Is there anyone else in there?' He
looked towards the girls, but they were not
taking any notice of him.

'I don't think so,' said Karl. 'These two
were against the back wall. There was some
junk in there, but nowhere anyone could
be hidden.'

'Should we check the house?' asked the
officer who had held Karl.

'Yeah, go on. Looks deserted, though.'

He turned back to Karl and Daniel.

'There'll be a fire engine here soon to put
this lot out. For now, though, I want you
and the girls over there by those bushes.
You'll be out of the way if it goes up.

There's an ambulance on the way, too.'

He carried on speaking, but his words were drowned out by the roaring thrum of the returning police helicopter overhead. Karl and Daniel looked up – it was low over them and they could see the pilot talking on his radio to the policeman, who was now back in the car. The helicopter rose quickly in to the air and banked off to the right. Further off, it descended and hovered, but Karl couldn't see what was happening. He turned to ask Daniel what he thought, but the policeman shepherded them towards the girls. The policeman went back to the car to get blankets for them, they were now shivering as well as crying. Daniel watched as the helicopter banked again and headed back in their direction.

Within moments there was too much

activity for Karl to see what was happening. The fire engine arrived and three firemen unravelled a hose which they took into the burning barn while a fourth shouted orders and moved everyone out of the way yet again, sending the girls to sit in one of the patrol cars. A few seconds later, the ambulance pulled up, siren blaring and lights flashing. Two paramedics in green suits jumped out and hurried over to the police car. And over the horizon came another police car, lights flashing but no siren. It swerved dramatically and screeched to a halt alongside the ambulance. The door opened and a police officer roughly dragged the two men out. They were handcuffed and sullen.

The policeman called Karl over.

'Recognise these guys?' he asked.

'Yes,' he said, then paused to cough.

'They're the ones who put me in the carpet. That blond one with eczema, he hit me and tied me up, the other gave the orders.'

The girls, wrapped in blankets, were escorted over by the paramedics.

'Did these men kidnap you?'

Eleni nodded. The other looked puzzled until Eleni translated, then she nodded too.

The officer who had driven the car Daniel was in turned on the two men.

'Why did you set fire to the building? You could have killed them. What was the sense in that?'

The dark man shrugged. The blond one spat on the ground and scowled at the girls, then spoke in broken English.

'Scum. They shouldn't be here. Their families – their village – it was our land. They took it. That one—' he pointed at Eleni 'she's just a gypsy. The other – her father and his brothers, they burned my village. My family died. Then I come here to start a new life. And again they are here. But this time I am in charge. This time—'

'Get in the car,' said the police officer holding the man's arms. 'Save your rant.'

'What were you going to do with them?' Karl said.

The policeman stopped pushing his prisoner for a moment.

'With them? I have a friend. He knows what to do with girls like that.'

'Like what?' asked Karl.

Vladan spat on the ground.

'Come on,' interrupted the policeman. 'Gossip time over. In you get.'

'They're scum. We sell them. Who cares?' Vladan shouted over his shoulder.

Eleni had moved next to Karl.

'He say "who cares"?'

'Yes,' said Karl, 'that's what he said.'

He turned to look at her. Dark hair blew across her face in the wind from the helicopter blades, now slow and lazy as they spun down. Her skin was brown from working in the sun, and smirched with mud and mascara. Her large eyes looked straight into his and he felt his stomach lurch.

'I care,' he said. With a thrill of surprise he felt her hand slip into his.

'Thank you,' she said. 'Do you remember me? I'm Eleni.'

'I do remember you. And this is Catarina? It's good to see you again,' he said, and laughed.

'You bet,' said Eleni. She was still holding his hand, and he didn't want her to let go. He squeezed her hand gently and she smiled, a glittering smile. No, he didn't want her to let go – not ever.

Look out for Dragonwood
by Alex Stewart

'I want you to bring me his head,' Lamiel
Silverthorn snarled, his elvish countenance
so twisted with loathing he could almost
have passed for human. Offhand, it was
hard to decide which of the two races would
have been most insulted at the comparison,
but Pip Summerdew cared little for the
feelings of either. They both tended to think
halflings like himself were little more than
gluttonous halfwits, to be treated with
amused condescension or barely veiled
contempt; which, on the whole, was a
distinct advantage in his line of work.

'Detaching it might prove a little difficult,'
Pip said, giving up trying to find a position
in the elven chair he was currently
occupying which allowed his feet to reach

the floor, and drawing them up to sit cross-legged instead.

A faint flicker of distaste crossed his host's visage as grubby bootsoles met exquisitely embroidered silk.

'I'm sure a bounty hunter of your experience can sort out the details.'

'Fair enough.' Pip nodded. Two hundred of the solid gold trade tokens the elves used when bartering with the merchants of other races would keep him in the style he hoped to become accustomed to for a very long time. 'Half up front, the rest when I deliver.'

Silverthorn's gold-flecked eyes narrowed a little, his thoughts as transparent as if he'd spoken them aloud. If Pip got himself killed before completing the assignment, he'd be well out of pocket, and no closer to the vengeance on his sister's murderer his honour demanded. 'I thought I'd pay you the full amount when you return with Graznik's head,' he said.

'Then you thought wrong,' Pip rejoined, hopping down to the polished oak floor. 'I'll see myself out.' He took a couple of paces towards the door.

'No. Wait.' Elves usually spoke in exquisitely modulated tones, which sounded more like choral music than normal speech to halfling and human ears, but Silverthorn's voice had begun to take on the timbre of someone treading on a cat. It was clear that the Prince of the Sylvan Marches wasn't used to being spoken to like this by anyone, least of all a scruffy little hairfoot. 'Half in advance, if you insist.'

'I do,' Pip said cheerfully. He waited while his host scribbled a note to the chief secretary of the Sylvan Marches embassy in Fennis, authorising the payment, and smiled sardonically. 'It won't turn into leaves when the sun comes up, will it?'

'That's fairy gold,' Silverthorn said shortly. 'Not ours. And even if it wasn't, I've got more sense than to try cheating someone in your profession.'

'Glad to hear it.' Pip slipped the note into his belt pouch. 'Any other instructions?'

'I thought I'd been clear enough,' Silverthorn said, a faint tic beginning to jump beside his right jaw. 'I want Graznik's head. What else is there to discuss?'

'Well,' Pip said slowly, 'your sister's body was never found. If it turns out she's alive after all, and still in the camp...'

'Ariella's dead,' Silverthorn said, in a tone which brooked no argument. 'The orcs of Dragonwood killed her. Can you carry out the assignment or not?'

Pip nodded.

'You have my word,' he said.

Any halfling with money in his purse would head for a tavern, as surely as water flowed downhill, although on this occasion Pip had another reason beyond the siren call of food and fine ale. The taproom was crowded, mainly with humans, but his reputation allowed him to proceed unimpeded to a discreet corner booth, where a corpulent young man in the robes of a wizard had already settled for the evening. He was dividing his attention roughly equally between the overflowing platter in front of him, the tankard of ale in his hand, and the serving wench at his elbow, who, despite the obvious glut of customers in need of her attention, was lingering to giggle at the display of coloured sparks dancing on the tabletop.

'Pip!' Kris the mage smiled a greeting to the halfling, murmured something inaudible to the girl, which made her blush, and dismissed the sparks with a wave of his hand. 'What'll you have?'

'I'll start with whatever you're having,' Pip said, clambering on to the opposite bench.

'Good choice,' Kris agreed, clearly contemplating dessert now Pip had arrived with a bulging purse. 'What can I do for you this time?'

'I need an edge,' Pip told him. 'Something like that Cloak of Shadows thing, but longer lasting. And something to muffle noise.'

'Not a problem.' Kris nodded, chewing thoughtfully at a chicken leg. 'But you don't usually need any help in sneaking about. Planning to walk through an army?' He grinned, amused at his own wit.

'Near enough,' Pip said, and began to eat.

Look out for these other great titles in the
Shades series:

Animal Lab
by Malcolm Rose

Jamie hates the fact he's
gone bald. But can it be
right that the animal lab
where he works is using
monkeys to find a cure?

Mind's Eye
by Gillian Philip

Braindeads like Conor
are scary. Or that's what
Lara used to think....

Four Degrees More
by Malcolm Rose

When Leyton Curry sees his house fall into the sea, there's nothing he can do...
Or is there?

Cuts Deep
by Catherine Johnson

Devon's heading for trouble till he meets Savannah, and starts to change. But can he ever put the past behind him?